JULIET RIX is an award-winning freelance writer and broadcaster, based in London. She started her career with BBC Television and Radio and writes for the *Guardian, Telegraph, Independent* and *The Times* as well as magazines and websites. She lives in north London.

JULIET SNAPE studied at Cambridge School of Art and completed with a post-graduate in illustration at St Martin's School of Art. Since then she has illustrated and written many picture books for children, including over 30 books with her husband, Charles. This is her first book for Frances Lincoln. She lives in north London.

Aberdeenshire

3165197

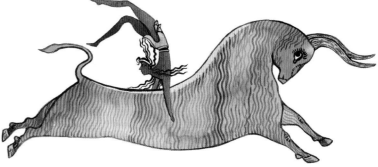

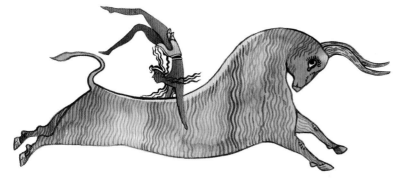

In memory of my father, and for my sons whose early enthusiasm
for mazes and myths sowed the seeds of this book. – J.R.

For Charles – J.S.

ABERDEENSHIRE
LIBRARIES

3165197

Bertrams	05/06/2015
JS	£7.99

JANETTA OTTER-BARRY BOOKS

Text copyright © Juliet Rix 2014
Illustrations copyright © Juliet Snape 2014
The rights of Juliet Rix and Juliet Snape to be identified respectively as the author and illustrator of this work have been
asserted by them in accordance with the Copyright, Designs and Patents Act, 1988 (United Kingdom).

First published in Great Britain and in the USA in 2014 by Frances Lincoln Children's Books

First published in paperback in Great Britain and in the USA in 2015 by
Frances Lincoln Children's Books
74-77 White Lion Street, London N1 9PF
www.franceslincoln.com

All rights reserved

No part of this publication may be reproduced, stored in a retrieval system,
or transmitted, in any form, or by any means, electrical, mechanical, photocopying, recording
or otherwise without the prior written permission of the publisher or a licence permitting
restricted copying. In the United Kingdom such licences are issued by the
Copyright Licensing Agency, Saffron House, 6-10 Kirby Street, London EC1N 8TS.

A catalogue record for this book is available from the British Library.

ISBN 978-1-84780-654-3

Illustrated with watercolour
Set in Albertus MT

Printed in China

1 3 5 7 9 8 6 4 2

A-MAZE-ING MINOTAUR

Written by JULIET RIX

Illustrated by JULIET SNAPE

Frances Lincoln
Children's Books

King Minos was a very powerful man – but he was not a very nice one. At his luxurious palace on the beautiful island of Crete, he kept a strange and dangerous beast. The Minotaur, part man, part bull, lived in a vast maze of narrow corridors and dark rooms – the Labyrinth. Once inside, no one could find their way out, or so it was believed. Every nine years, King Minos fed the Minotaur a terrible meal: fourteen young people, seven boys and seven girls, brought across the water from Athens. The Athenians didn't want to send their children to die, but they didn't dare defy King Minos.

Theseus, Prince of Athens, was just the right age to be sent to Crete. To the horror of his father, the king, he insisted on going.

"I will kill the Minotaur," he declared.

Theseus and the other young Athenians set sail, and were greeted in Crete by King Minos himself.

"You have one night left to live," he said. "Feast and make merry. Tomorrow you go into the Labyrinth."

At the king's side was a beautiful girl. Theseus noticed her immediately – and she could not take her eyes off Theseus. Her name was Ariadne and she was King Minos's daughter.

Later that night, when the palace was quiet, Ariadne found Theseus alone. He was desperately trying to work out a plan. How could he kill the Minotaur with his bare hands? And how would he find his way out of the Labyrinth?

"I can help you," said Ariadne.

At first Theseus was suspicious. Ariadne was Minos's daughter, after all. But the princess had fallen in love with Theseus and she convinced him that she too feared her father's cruelty.

Ariadne gave Theseus a sword, small enough to hide in his tunic, and a ball of golden thread. "Unravel it as you go into the Labyrinth," she said, "and you will always be able to find your way out." She promised to be at the door of the maze when Theseus returned.

Theseus fell asleep with the golden ball clutched to his heart.

The next day, with great fanfare, the young Athenians were taken to the Labyrinth. The Cretans watched, certain that these young people would never be seen again. The heavy doors to the maze swung open. Theseus and his friends were thrust inside and the doors clanged shut behind them.

It was dark in the Labyrinth and the youngsters shivered with fear. But Theseus went straight into action. He tied the golden thread to the Labyrinth door and told his friends, "You must wait here until I return." They protested that he should not go alone, but Theseus was resolute. "I am Prince of Athens," he said. "It is my job to get you safely away from here."

So Theseus set off into the Labyrinth, the golden ball in one hand, Ariadne's sword in the other.

He stepped slowly in the darkness, carefully unravelling the golden thread.

There were so many corridors, so many corners. Sometimes Theseus met a dead end, or went right round in a circle and nearly tripped over his own golden thread.

His heart was pounding, but he knew he had to be brave. He had the sword and the golden thread. His friends depended on him. Ariadne believed in him. He must end the terror of the Minotaur.

So on he went, unwinding the thread behind him, alert for any sound of the monster.

It happened in an instant. Suddenly the Minotaur was towering over him, his bull's head staring down with bulging eyes.

Theseus dropped the golden thread and lashed out with his sword. The Minotaur opened his great mouth and Theseus went at him with all his might. The Minotaur let out a mighty roar and Theseus screamed. Bull's hair met boy's skin, sword struck horn, arms and legs flailed everywhere...

Then all went quiet.

The Minotaur slumped. Theseus stood back. The terrifying monster lay still.

Theseus waited, uncertain, over the body of the beast. He looked down at his own body. His leg was bleeding, but it was only a scratch.

He was alive and the Minotaur was dead!

Theseus let out a long sigh of relief and turned to look for the golden thread. He couldn't see it. He felt along the ground behind him – nothing but hard stone. He began to panic. Without the thread, how would he find his way out of the Labyrinth?

At last his hand caught on the final twists of the golden thread, lying where he had dropped them. Slowly but surely, he wound the thread in, carefully retracing his steps through the maze. The Labyrinth was just as eerie as before, but Theseus was no longer afraid.

The delight on the faces of his thirteen friends was
something Theseus remembered for the rest of his life.
But they were not safe yet. Together they knocked on
the great doors of the Labyrinth. Would Ariadne be there?

The locks slid back. Theseus pushed, and the great doors
swung open. The smiling princess put her finger to her lips
and pointed the way to the sea.

Quickly and quietly, Theseus and Ariadne and their Athenian friends ran to where their ship lay waiting. Swiftly they boarded, silently they loosed the ropes and the ship moved soundlessly away.

Not a word passed their lips, but they could see the joy in each other's eyes as Theseus and Ariadne embraced. Never again would King Minos take the lives of young Athenians to feed his monstrous Minotaur.

The truth behind the story

Crete is one of the Greek islands, and on the outskirts of the modern capital, Heraklion, you can visit the remains of Knossos, the centre of Minoan civilisation. The buildings here were excavated by the British archaeologist Sir Arthur Evans, who believed them to be the remains of the Palace of Minos.

The story of the Minotaur is a myth, but the Minoans were real enough and they ruled Crete for 1500 years, from around 5000 years ago. They built great palaces and towns across the island, the remains of which can still be seen today.

No Labyrinth has been found at Knossos, but excavations have revealed a vast complex of buildings with a large central courtyard reached by an angled corridor and surrounded by over 1000 interconnecting rooms. Could the palace itself have been 'the Labyrinth'?

Archaeologists have also uncovered fragments of Minoan paintings on the walls at Knossos (the originals are now in the Heraklion Museum) and at other Minoan sites on Crete. The pictures in this book were inspired by the Minoan style of art and architecture.

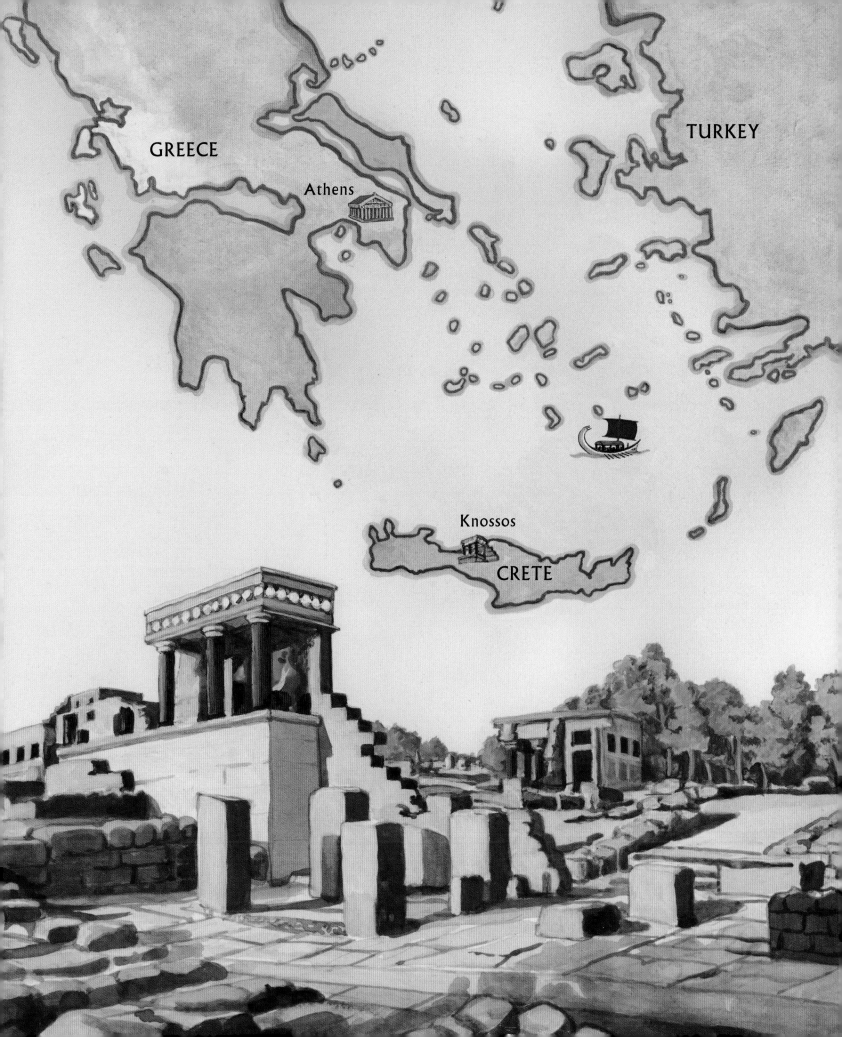

GREECE

Athens

TURKEY

Knossos

CRETE

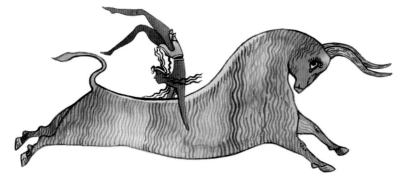
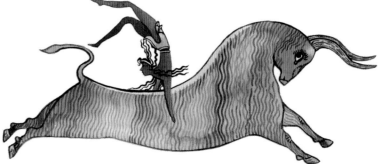

More picture books about ancient Greece from Frances Lincoln Children's Books

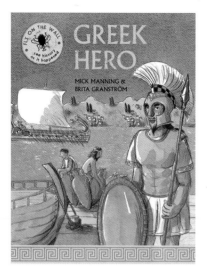

978-1-84780-622-2

Fly on the Wall: Greek Hero
Written by and illustrated by
Mick Manning and Brita Ganström

Be a fly on the wall in the time of the ancient Greeks. Follow Greek warrior Agathon on his way home from battle, listen to Ariston tell tales of brave Odysseus, learn Alpha to Omega with mischievous Hektor and hear the crowd roar as you watch Olympic athletes sprint for the finishing-line. These pages are packed with up-to-date information about the world of the ancient Greeks from the latest archaeological discoveries, so you can see history as it really happened!

"…has an energy and a warmth which really brings history to life." — *Books for Keeps*

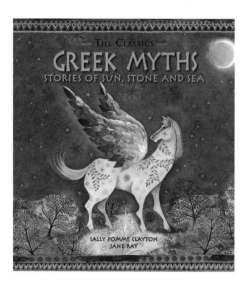

978-1-84780-508-9

**Greek Myths:
Stories of Sun, Stone and Sea**
Written by Sally Pomme Clayton
Illustrated by Jane Ray

Atalanta, Medusa, Perseus, Pandora, Pegasus — the very names conjure up an ancient world of wonder. These ten spellbinding tales from Greek mythology, accompanied by glowing illustrations from the award-winning illustrator, Jane Ray, are perfect for reading aloud to younger children. The collection includes a map showing places in Greece that are connected with the stories.

"The fabled world of ancient Greece comes alive through these ten myths that feature some of the most powerful gods, fearless heroes and amazing animals in literature."
— *Kirkus Review*

Frances Lincoln titles are available from all good bookshops.
You can also buy books and find out more about your favourite titles,
authors and illustrators on our website: www.franceslincoln.com